The Boyne Valley

book of

IRISH LEGENDS

Text: Brenda Maguire

Illustrations: Peter Haigh

Stories on tape read by

Gay Byrne · Cyril Cusack · Maureen Potter

John B. Keane · Rosaleen Linehan · Twink

LUCKY TREE BOOKS

THE O'BRIEN PRESS

Contents

First published 1987 by The O'Brien Press Ltd.,
20 Victoria Road, Dublin 6, Ireland.
Copyright ©. text, illustrations and tape: Boyne Valley Honey Company.
ISBN 0-86278-140-X

Book and cover design: Michael O'Brien. Editing: Ide O'Leary.
Typesetting: Design and Art Facilities, Dublin.
Printing: Leinster Leader Ltd., Naas.

The stories you are going to hear are old, old tales. They were told in Ireland long ago by storytellers who were called shanachies. These storytellers were very important people in Ireland then. Only the king was more important! The storytellers sat at the king's table, they wore cloaks of many colours and they kept large herds of cattle to show just how important and wealthy they were. Some of them stayed all their lives with one family or clan. Others travelled around from clan to clan, telling their stories in each place. Everybody looked forward to the arrival of the storyteller. Now they would hear new stories! The storyteller was always welcome.

These storytellers of old knew hundreds of stories. Many tales would take two or three nights to tell — stories of wonderful adventures, of magic steeds, fearsome giants and hags, mountains made of glass, palaces of gold, stories of beautiful maidens, stories of ghosts and fairies and leprechauns . . .

One of the oldest and best-loved stories tells of Cúchulainn, the great Ulster warrior.

Cúchulainn

Cúchulainn was of noble birth. His uncle was Conor Mac Nessa, King of Ulster. Conor lived in a palace at Emain Macha, near where Armagh is today.

A troop of expert soldiers, known as the Red Branch Knights, defended Ulster for Conor Mac Nessa. They were known throughout the length and breadth of Ireland, and people spoke in hushed tones of their great and fearless deeds.

The warriors of the Red Branch Knights began their training at an early age when they joined the Machra. The Machra was a troop of boys who were trained by King Conor himself at Emain Macha.

Cúchulainn grew up in a house built of oak wood in a place called Cooley, in County Louth. From an early age he had heard many stories of the heroic deeds of the Red Branch Knights, and he longed to become a warrior of Ulster.

When he was still only five years old Cúchulainn begged his mother to allow him travel to Emain Macha to join the Machra. She felt he was far too young to leave home and make the long journey on foot, alone. But Cúchulainn was a child of great strength and skill and he was very good at getting his own way, and, finally, his mother agreed to let him go. So, taking his hurley, his silver ball, his javelin and his toy spear he set out for his uncle's palace.

The road stretched northwards over the mountains where only wild animals lived. But Cúchulainn was never lonely, for when news reached his woodland friends that he was travelling their way, they came out to keep him company.

A black-eared rabbit, with four white paws, played hide-and-seek with him along the road. And a sleek-haired fox, with a bushy tail, trotted along beside him for several miles; they whiled away the time solving riddles and conundrums and brain-twisters, but though no child of his own age could equal Cúchulainn, he was no match for the fox!

When the fox reached the boundary of his territory and left

Cúchulainn to return to his den, the small birds of the air flew low overhead to show the young boy the way to Emain Macha.

To shorten the journey Cúchulainn would hit the silver ball with the hurley, and then leap forward and hit it a second time before it reached the ground, then he would toss the javelin ahead and lastly the spear, and then run after them all, pick up the ball

and the javelin with one hand, and before the spear's tip could touch the ground he would catch it with his other hand.

When Cúchulainn reached Emain Macha, one hundred and fifty young boys were playing hurling and practising martial arts on the playing fields beside Conor's palace. Eager to show off his own skills, Cúchulainn dived in among the boys. He caught the ball, ran the length of the field with it, outstripping even the fastest amongst them, and he sent it home into the goal.

Well! The boys were very angry. Who was this stranger who had joined in their game without being asked? They attacked him from all sides. They threw their sticks at his head, but he twisted and dodged. They flung their javelins at his body, but he stopped them with his toy shield. No one could touch him. And then, Cúchulainn made an onslaught on them! He laid low fifty boys and chased another fifty from the field.

Conor Mac Nessa and Fergus Mac Roy were playing chess nearby. King Conor noticed the skill and courage of this young child. Who was he? When he learned that Cúchulainn was his own nephew, Conor ordered the boys to make peace with him, and invited Cúchulainn to join the Machra.

When he was a boy, Cúchulainn's name was Setanta, and he would have been pleased to keep that name for life, but fate stepped in to change it. It happened like this.

Shortly after Setanta joined the Machra, King Conor and his chieftains were invited to a feast at the fort of Cullen, the smith.

Setanta was chosen to go with them. This was a great honour, because Cullen was widely known for his skill in making spears and swords for the great warriors of Ulster.

However, when King Conor was leaving Emain Macha for Cullen's fort, Setanta was playing a game of hurling, so it was agreed that he would follow on afterwards when the game was finished.

Now, like many forts at that time, Cullen's fort was surrounded by a bank of beaten earth, with a stone wall set on top. Inside, around the low-lying buildings, was space for the cattle that were driven in each night to protect them from wild animals or from marauding armies.

Cullen welcomed King Conor and his party, and when they were safely inside the fort he locked and bolted the great wooden door in the wall and he let loose his fierce watchdog. Everyone forgot that Setanta had not yet arrived!

'My hound has the strength of a hundred hounds,' boasted Cullen. 'He is the cruellest, the fiercest, the most savage dog alive. No one has ever dared pass him by —

and lived to tell the tale!'

Well, it was almost dark when the game of hurling was over. Setanta's team won the match and he was in high good humour as he neared Cullen's fort. He hadn't eaten since morning, so his mind was on beef broth, succulent roast boar, wild strawberries and cream, wheaten cakes cooked in honey . . . .

A long, piercing howl woke him from his thoughts. In the moonlight he saw two angry yellow eyes staring at him. Setanta felt a moment of panic. The hound had taken him by surprise, and his only means of defence was his hurley and ball. With one

bound the animal charged, jaws open, fangs ready to tear the boy apart, limb from limb. Setanta lifted his hurley and with great force he hurled the ball into the dog's open mouth and straight down his throat. The unfortunate animal gave a yelp of pain, turned somersault and his lifeless body fell with a great crash to the ground.

The pitiful baying of the hound passed like lightning through the banqueting hall where the visitors had gathered. And then King Conor remembered Setanta. Fearing that the little boy had been torn to pieces, Conor rushed from the hall, sword at the ready, and ordered the gates to be opened. He saw his nephew, shaken but unharmed, standing over the dead hound. King Conor was full of praise and joy.

But Cullen did not share the King's joy. With a lump in his throat and a tear in his eye the smith gathered the dead dog in his arms.

'Oh,' he wept, 'I have lost a friend. There was not his equal for faithfulness or bravery in all Ireland. Who will guard my fort now?'

Well, Setanta saw Cullen's grief and he spoke up. He said, 'I killed your dog because I had no choice. But give me a pup of this hound and I will train him to be the equal of the dog I have killed. And until then I shall guard your fort myself.'

Setanta kept his word, and from that day forward Setanta was known as Cú Chulainn, the Hound of Cullen.

In time Cúchulainn became leader of the Machra and later of the Red Branch Knights. He led them through many fierce battles until he died facing his enemies, tied to a standing stone on the plains of Muirthemne in County Louth.

The Salmon of Knowledge

In the third century a very wise and powerful High King, named Cormac Mac Airt, lived at Tara in County Meath. Cormac had a band of warriors called the Fianna, who fought his enemies in time of war. In time of peace they hunted wild boar and red deer in the fierce forests and fertile valleys of Ireland. And they entertained the High King in the great hall at Tara with sweet music, poetry and wonderful stories of their heroic exploits.

The great Fionn Mac Cumhaill — the fair-haired son of Cumhall — was the Fianna's most famous leader.

When Fionn was a tiny baby in the cradle, his father, Cumhall, was killed in battle. Fionn's mother knew that it would be just a matter of time before her young son was sought out and killed by his father's enemies. So, although it broke her heart, she courageously said goodbye to her baby and gave him into the care of two wise women warriors who lived deep in a wood on the slopes of Sliabh Bloom, in County Laois.

Fionn was lonely for home and he missed his mother, but the women were kind and gentle and loving. By day they taught him how to hunt and fish, and to fight with sling and sword and spear, and at night they lulled him to sleep with strange and wonderful music on the harp.

The wise women of Sliabh Bloom fired Fionn's imagination with wild and marvellous stories of the Fianna and as he grew to manhood he became more and more determined to take his rightful place as leader of the Fianna.

Fionn had few companions during his growing years, but his faithful dog, Bran, was always at his heels. Fionn and Bran had a secret place, under the shade of an old oak tree, and there Fionn would dream his dreams of the future.

'My brave Bran, when I am leader of the Fianna you will be my most trusted hound. You and I will hunt rabbit and wolf, hare

and deer, badger and boar. Together we will scale the highest mountains, ford the swiftest rivers; we will outrun the wind, the swallow and the deer, and towards evening, when the sun is setting in the west, we will set the sky ablaze with our bonfires. We will lie back on the warm earth and listen to the crackle of the roasting meat and watch the sweet juices hiss and spit on the leaping flames.' And Bran would nuzzle up close to his master and lick his face.

When the wise women of Sliabh Bloom had taught Fionn all they knew and could teach him no more, they bade him farewell, and he set out for the beautiful Boyne valley, where the wisest men in Ireland lived.

Fionn went to live with and learn from Finneigeas, a poet of great genius, who lived on the banks of the Boyne. Finneigeas was a kindly man, eighty years old. He had two passions in life — poetry and fishing.

By day he would wade out into the river Boyne and cast his line in the hope of hooking a brown trout or a silver salmon. By night he would sit at an open fire and tell Fionn poems and stories from his endless collection.

Finneigeas had long heard of the heroic deeds of Fionn's father and he was well pleased to teach this fair-haired, blue-eyed youth all he knew. And Fionn grew to love the old man.

Under Finneigeas's expert guidance, Fionn soon mastered all the mysteries of poetry. Finneigeas cared little for his own well-being, so Fionn kept him supplied with fresh meat and wild berries, and when the poet's throat became hoarse from too much talk, Fionn would cure it with a soothing mixture of honey and hot fruit juice.

Finneigeas often told Fionn about the Salmon of Knowledge. For seven long years Finneigeas had dreamed of catching the Salmon. This magic fish lived in the river Boyne and it was said that the first person to taste the Salmon would receive the gift of wisdom and the power to see into the future.

Finneigeas tried every trick and every skill he knew to hook the fish, but all in vain. Time and again the silvery body twisted and turned, but always escaped just in time. Once, the poet did hook the salmon, but before he could land it, the fish broke free and swam to safety, with the hook still embedded in its skin. This, however, only made Finneigeas more determined than ever to succeed.

One perfect summer day the sun was high in a clear blue sky. Far away the lark spilled out its song to the clear air. Fionn lay on the grassy banks of the Boyne trying to remember the best poems his master had taught him. He dreamt of a supper of nuts and apples and wild strawberries and cream, and roasted salmon drowned with honey.

Bran was nowhere to be seen. He loved to frolic about in the cool waters of the Boyne, but today Finneigeas had scolded him for upsetting his fishing, and the dog, tail between his legs, had scurried off to vent his feelings on some unfortunate rabbit or hare.

Suddenly, a deafening whoop of delight startled Fionn and he jumped up — to be half drowned by an almighty splash. Finneigeas had hooked the Salmon of Knowledge and this time there was no escape!

Fionn ran to his master's side and helped draw in the twisting silvery body and unhook the line.

'Oh joy, oh rapture,
my treasure I capture,'
said Finneigeas. It wasn't his best effort at poetry, but excitement had made him lightheaded.

Indeed, the fish was beautiful to behold, Fionn thought, the biggest salmon he had ever laid eyes on, with a body like silver, scales like jewels and flesh of the richest pink.

In great excitement Fionn heated the stones in the pit to cook the fish, while his master danced around him warning him not to taste even a morsel. Whoever was first to taste the Salmon would gain all its knowledge. After all his long years of effort, Finneigeas wanted to be first.

Fionn laughed and agreed, and set about cleaning the fish and preparing it for the cooking pit. Bran, whose curiosity had been aroused by the commotion, was now running around in circles barking at a butterfly and falling over the twigs for the kindling.

With great ceremony Fionn rubbed the Salmon with wild garlic and placed it on cabbage leaves on the red-hot stones. Finneigeas was wild with excitement. Soon the delicious aroma of cooking was wafted through the air. Carefully Fionn turned and basted the fish, so that it would be succulent to taste and perfectly cooked.

As often happens in cooking, a blister rose on the back of the Salmon and, without a thought, Fionn firmly pressed down the rising, sizzling skin with his thumb. Again, as often happens, he put his burnt thumb into his mouth to soothe it — and then his head began to spin.

Fionn garnished the cooked Salmon with wild parsley, anointing it with honey, and set it before the poet. But something strange was happening to Fionn — and the poet knew it.

'Thoughts are racing through my mind like clouds on a windy day. I can see . . .' Fionn stopped, dismayed. And the poet said, sadly, 'You ate the first portion of the Salmon.'

'I did not,' Fionn said, but already he knew, and the poet knew. 'I burnt my thumb on the flesh of the fish and sucked the burn.'

The old man let out a great sigh. 'You have tasted the Salmon of Knowledge. It was written in the stars that you should. From this day forth all knowledge is yours. You are the wisest of men. I can teach you no more. It's right that Fionn, the leader of the Fianna, should have the gift of wisdom.'

As for Bran — he thought Fionn's new-found gift was a mixed blessing. He'll always know where I am and save me if I'm in danger, and this is good, Bran thought. But, he'll also know when I'm chasing cats or hens or that tiresome donkey on the hill. And, never again can I pretend not to hear him when he calls me!

Oisín in Tír na nÓg the Land of Youth

Long before St Patrick came to Ireland, our ancestors believed in a happy Otherworld, called Tír na nÓg, the Land of Youth, far out in the Atlantic Ocean. Ordinary human beings were sometimes allowed to visit this land. It was an island paradise where nobody ever became old! Oisín was the son of Fionn Mac Cumhail, leader of the Fianna warriors. Now, Oisín had always longed to visit Tír na nÓg, the land beyond all dreams. His wish was granted one dewy May morning when he was hunting with Fionn and the Fianna among the mist-covered hills that surround Lough Lein in the County Kerry.

The hedges were heavy with fragrance of hawthorn, and, high above, the little birds sang sweetly on the branches of the tall oak trees. But on the ground all was quiet. Not even a rabbit moved.

Suddenly, a snow-white fawn bounded from a thicket and ran before the hounds. Oisín loved a chase and, with Bran and Sceolan his faithful hounds in full cry, he soon outstripped the men and dogs of the Fianna.

The fawn led them a merry dance along winding mountain paths, through deep valleys, across swollen rivers and through thick forests until, at last, they came to a plain near a sheltered bay in west Kerry.

Bran and Sceolan were gaining on the fawn when the animal suddenly disappeared behind a hawthorn bush. Just as suddenly a fairy mist moved in from the sea and wafted towards them. As the mist neared Oisín it lifted, and a beautiful girl on a milk-white horse rode towards them.

She wore a gown of sea-green silk, which was spangled with stars of brightest blue. Her golden hair fell around her shoulders like a priceless cloak and on her head she wore a crown richly studded with rubies and pearls.

Her white horse was covered with a smooth-flowing mantle of purple and gold. His hooves were shod with shoes of shining silver and his golden bridle glistened in the rising sun.

Oisín had never seen or imagined anyone so beautiful. The girl looked at him, smiling.

Oisín took courage and asked, 'Who are you, o beautiful maiden? And how can I be of service to you?'

'I am Niamh of the Golden Hair,' she answered. 'I am the daughter of the King of Tír na nÓg. Your fame, Oisín, as a poet and a warrior has spread to the Land of Youth and I have come to take you home with me. In Tír na nÓg you will know neither death nor sorrow. It is a land of joy and happiness, where the trees bear fruit the whole year through and where there is always plenty of honey and wine.'

Oisín listened, bewitched, as Niamh told him of the wonders of her homeland, of the wealth and fame that awaited him and of her love for him. Then, still in a dream, Oisín moved towards Niamh and mounted the horse behind her.

The white horse shook his mane and wheeled round to go. Bran and Sceolan, who had up to now stood spellbound at Oisín's heels, raised their heads in grief, a yowl that was echoed by Fionn and the Fianna who had just come into sight.

As the fairy horse and its riders neared the west coast, the sea

opened up before them, and Oisín cast one last look at Fionn and the Fianna and the green shores of Ireland.

The journey to Tír na nÓg was strange and wonderful. Away, far away they rode, farther than I could tell you and twice as far as you could tell me. They passed marble cities, glinting golden castles; they overtook the wind before them, and the wind behind them could not overtake them.

Once a slender doe crossed their path, chased by a snow-white hound. Then followed a chariot carrying a youth in knightly dress and a young girl bouncing a sparkling ball. Oisín wondered at these marvellous sights but Niamh assured him they were as nothing compared to the delights that awaited him in Tír na nÓg.

At long last they came to a land most beautiful to behold. Green plains, blue hills and bright lakes and waterfalls stretched for miles on every side. The sun shone down and strange, colourful butterflies fluttered lazily from flower to flower. A shimmering stream ran down the hill and Oisín could see silver fish leap in the air. He clapped his hands and an apple fell from a tree.

A clear path led to a lowered drawbridge, beside which stood two lines of guardsmen. Even amongst the mighty warriors of the Fianna, Oisín had never seen such fearsome men. Yet, when he drew alongside them, he could sense that they meant no harm. Then, all together, they saluted their princess, Niamh.

As if glad to be home, the white horse moved swiftly over the moat and into a cobbled courtyard. A tall, thin groom, immaculately dressed, took the reins and a footman helped Niamh and Oisín dismount.

Oisín and Niamh silently followed a procession of servants

into the palace where a fanfare of trumpets greeted their arrival. Oisín had never seen such a fantastic room, not even when he visited the High King of Ireland at royal Tara.

A hundred courtiers were seated at the long oak tables. They drank from golden goblets and ate from plates of coral. A red carpet ran from Oisín's feet through the hall and up to two ivory thrones. Niamh moved forward and Oisín followed, his feet never touching the ground as he floated through the air. He wondered at this, and then remembered he was in Tír na nÓg, the magical land.

'Welcome, Oisín, son of Fionn,' said the King, in a voice which filled the hall. 'We have watched your progress across the seas and through the mists of time. The prophecy of the sages has been fulfilled.'

The Queen bent forward and joined Oisín's and Niamh's hands, and the entire court raised a mighty cheer. Bells rang out as Oisín and Niamh were wed. Such splendour has never been seen before or since. The feasting lasted a week, and the last day was better than the first.

Three years went quickly by and in all that time Oisín never gave thought to Fionn or his companions in the Fianna, or to the chase or to the company around the camp-fire. That is, until one day he found a shamrock holding a drop of water like a tear in its heart, and memory came flooding back.

'I must return to Ireland at once for a visit,' he told Niamh.

'If you wish to go, there is nothing I can do to hold you,' she said. 'You must follow where your heart leads.'

She walked with him to where her favourite mount was stabled.

'The white horse brought you here,' said Niamh. 'He will take you back. But, be warned — do not dismount. Never get down off your horse, because if you do I shall never see you again.'

The people of Tír na nÓg were sad to see Oisín leave and there was a lump in Oisín's throat as the white horse carried him over the waves. But when they arrived on the shores of Kerry his sadness turned to joy. Soon he would see all his old companions once again!

Swiftly the white steed raced across Ireland. Dawn was breaking when they reached the Hill of Allen where the Fianna camped — but now all was changed. Overgrown weeds and nettles were silent witnesses that no one had passed that way for many years. Oisín's heart sank, but he tried to cheer himself up.

'They must have moved camp,' he reassured his horse.

Throughout the days that followed, Oisín scoured the countryside, searching in vain for his comrades, and then, one

morning, as he rode into Gleann na Smól, just beyond Bohernabreena in County Wicklow, he saw two young men trying to move a boulder. Compared to the mighty Fianna they looked puny and weak. Oisín bent towards them and they came timidly forward.

'Have you seen Fionn and the Fianna?' he asked.

One man scuffed the ground in silence. His companion scratched his head in wonder.

'My grandfather had a story from his grandfather how once the noble Fionn hunted the wild boar,' he said.

They turned back to their task, sweating and straining, and in pity Oisín stooped from his saddle and with a mighty heave tossed the boulder into the air. As he did so the golden girth on the white horse snapped and Oisín was sent tumbling to the ground. A mist swam before his eyes. His strength was ebbing and his body shrivelling and, before the disbelieving eyes of the two young men, the mighty Oisín turned into an old, old man. He knew then what had happened. Three hundred years had passed since he had left Ireland. In Tír na nÓg a hundred years was the same as a year and now those years had caught up with him.

Across the glen a church bell was chiming and when Oisín heard that Ireland was now Christian he asked that the holy Patrick be brought to him. He told the saint of his days with Fionn and the Fianna and of his time with Niamh in Tír na nÓg, and the saint's scribe wrote the stories down on parchment lest they be forgotten. Then Patrick baptised Oisín and closed his eyes for the last time.

Sometimes, away on the western seaboard, fishermen and children point out a misty island which they say is the Land of Youth, but for all that no one ever saw the white steed or the beautiful Niamh again.

The Mysterious Beggarman

Long ago in Ireland, before Patrick lit the Easter fire at Tara and converted the Irish to Christianity, the gods often came out of the hollow hills and helped heroes and champions, especially the young. Perhaps the best-known and best-loved of these gods was Aengus. He might suddenly appear in any shape or form — as he did one mysterious day when the hunt brought Fionn and the Fianna to the Hill of Howth, in north County Dublin, and danger threatened from the terrible magician, Caol an Iarainn, of the Eastern World.

It was November Eve, when the unseen world, which is all around us, draws near. Fionn and his men had camped on Howth Hill for the night. Now, with the first light of dawn, they were assembled down at the harbour with horses and dogs, all eager for a day's hunting which would take them half way across Ireland.

A thick, grey mist covered the sea and, as it lifted, the Fianna saw a ship, with full-blown sails, move into the bay. A tall man, of magnificent build, dressed in a cloak of scarlet caught up by a great golden brooch, swung from the side of the boat by means of a spear. With one bound he was across the beach to where the Fianna were gathered.

Fionn raised a hand in greeting. 'Welcome, stranger. I am Fionn and these are my companions.'

'A poor bunch, fit only for hunting rabbits and hedgehogs,' the stranger growled, and with that he tore off his helmet and threw it at Fionn's feet.

'I, Caol an Iarainn, son of the King of Thessaly, challenge your best runner to a contest — the winner to take the gold, chariots, horses and the dogs of the Fianna.'

Silence followed this unexpected demand. Caol an Iarainn had spoken so harshly and stared with such an evil eye that dismay seized the Fianna. Even Fionn held his breath.

At last Fionn spoke. 'Caoilte Mac Ronán is our champion runner. He will accept your challenge. But he is on his way to Tara to tell the High King we shall spend the night with him. If you agree to come hunting with us today, I promise you a good contest tomorrow.'

'The race will take place now. Immediately! At once!' the stranger bullied.

Once, long ago, Fionn had burnt his thumb on the Salmon of Knowledge. This gave him great wisdom, and now he chewed his thumb and made a wish: Let me pick someone who can beat this arrogant stranger.

'That someone is me,' said a voice in his ear, and standing before Fionn was a clumsy, ugly-looking fellow in a mud-spattered, ill-fitting coat, which flapped against the calves of his big, misshapen legs.

Fionn put an arm on the Beggarman's shoulder. 'Our friend here will take up the challenge. He will race against Caol an Iarainn.'

The Fianna hooted with laughter, and small wonder why! The Beggarman could hardly walk, let alone run, and when he lifted a foot the boot on the end of it squelched with the weight of mud that clung to the sole.

Caol an Iarainn grew purple in the face. 'I will not raise a foot to race a great clumsy clod of a beggarman.' But before he could utter another word the Beggarman had him pinned down in the sand.

'You'll accept my offer or I'll knock you and your boat to the end of the world. What distance did you have in mind?'

'I never run less than two hundred miles,' choked Caol.

'A small trot, but it'll do,' the Beggarman said, grinning. 'From this place to Sliabh Luachra is two hundred miles. We can meander down there today and in the morning start our race from Sliabh Luachra back here to the Hill of Howth.'

The odd-looking pair set out on their journey, and at long last they reached Sliabh Luachra.

'I'm allergic to night air,' the Beggarman wheezed. 'We had better build a house to pass the night.'

'You'll get no help from me,' Caol said gruffly, and looked at the Beggarman as if he had as many heads as coats, and with that he settled himself down in the hollow of an old oak tree and fell fast asleep.

The Beggarman uprooted trees as easily as if they were

thistles and, in no time, had built a snug, well-timbered house and lit an enormous fire.

'I'm famished with the hunger,' the Beggarman said and cocked a grinning eye at Caol. 'Will you help me search for food?'

Caol was not amused. 'Search yourself and let me sleep. But if you run into danger I'll not lift a finger to help you.'

'Then supperless you shall be this night.' And, with that, the Beggarman disappeared into the darkness of the forest. He returned with a fine pig over his shoulder and soon the sizzling and crackling and the tantalising smell of succulent roast pork wafted across to where Caol an Iarainn was sleeping and maddened him with hunger.

When the Beggarman had eaten his fill, he settled himself down on a bed of soft rushes and fell fast asleep.

Dawn was breaking when Caol poked the Beggarman roughly in the ribs. 'Get up, you lazy good-for-nothing,' he hissed, 'it's time we were on our way.'

'I never surface until the sun has dried the dew. If you are in such a hurry, start running. I'll trot behind you in an hour or two.' And the Beggarman turned over and went to sleep again.

The next time the Beggarman woke the sun was high in the heavens and a stray goat was nuzzling him gently. He milked the goat and finished the remains of the previous night's supper. Then he tied the bones in the tail of his coat and set off for the Hill of Howth.

He ran in a most bewildering manner. Sometimes he moved backwards, a lot of the time he ran sideways and most of the time he just seemed to dance a jig where he was. But for all that he outpaced the red deer and left the swallows far behind and in no time at all he had caught up with Caol an Iarainn.

'I saved you some breakfast,' the Beggarman chuckled, and tossed him a few bones. 'You look as if you could do with some nourishment.'

'Keep your filthy bones,' Caol shouted, red with anger. His clothes were soaked in sweat. 'I'd rather die of starvation than eat your leavings.'

'You're not even making an effort to win,' the Beggarman taunted. 'Try running like this.'

With one bound the Beggarman was over the hill and into the next valley before the weary Caol could draw breath.

'The hunger is slowing me down,' the Beggarman said, rubbing his stomach. 'I fancy a nice piece of fish.' He waded into

the middle of a fast-running river and, in less time than it takes to tell, he had caught and cooked a fine brown trout.

The Beggarman was stretched out resting after his meal when Caol arrived.

'You left the tail of your coat on a bramble bush twenty miles back,' Caol grunted. 'The stench from it has frightened the animals away.'

The Beggarman sighed. 'Oh dear, I'd better get it. I don't like to upset my woodland friends.'

He ran backwards and, when at last he found the bush, he recovered his coat tail and sewed it back on. Then he stripped the bush bare of blackberries and when he had eaten his fill and could eat no more he took off his coat and stuffed the pockets, the sleeves and the lining with blackberries. He slung the soggy bundle over his shoulder and set his course for Howth.

Fionn had despaired of ever seeing his mysterious friend again when the Fianna let out a great whoop of joy. The Beggarman had just somersaulted on to the beach, and, far behind him, losing ground, came Caol an Iarainn. The Fianna went galloping and rolling and jumping down the hill to the strand, cheering and thumping and walloping each other with sheer relief. They tried to lift the Beggarman shoulder high, but he was emptying out the blackberries and crushing them into the sand.

From the top of the hill, Fionn watched Caol, sword drawn, face contorted, make a sudden lunge at the Beggarman. But just as quickly a great ball of blackberry mess came through the air and hit Caol full in the face. When Fionn looked again he saw Caol an Iarainn's head bouncing about on the sand like a football!

'I'd best do the decent thing,' the Beggarman muttered. 'Sure my heart is as soft as butter.' And with that, he picked up the head and flung it at the body, where it stuck on back to front!

The last anyone saw of Caol an Iarainn was when he was running across the beach, towards the boat, his feet pointing out to sea and his face grimacing back at the Fianna.

As for the Beggarman, he was nowhere to be seen. But the air was filled with magic music and a fairy mist curled and spiralled and wafted across the beach and was lost out to sea. Fionn heaved a deep sigh and raised his hand in a farewell salute to the great god Aengus, who had come to help the Fianna in their hour of need.

The Children of Lir

Once upon a time, and a very good time it was, there lived in Ireland a wise and noble king, called Bov the Red. Bov had a daughter called Eve, a girl of rare beauty and charm. When Eve was eighteen years old she fell in love with and married Lir, a chieftain of a strange tribe of people called the Tuatha de Danann.

Lir lived at his fort at Shee Finnaha, just beyond the Gap of the North, leading to Ulster. Eve loved her new home, and their happiness was complete when Eve gave birth to twin children — a sweet and lovely daughter whom they called Fionnuala, and a handsome and gentle son named Aodh. Some years later two boys, Fiachra and Conn, were born, and Lir's happiness knew no bounds.

Then, tragedy struck. When Fiachra and Conn were still toddlers, Eve died. Lir was heartbroken, and he too would have died but for the great love he had for his children.

The children missed their mother very much, but they tried every trick they knew to make their father happy. They filled the house with wild woodbine, scarlet fuchsia and yellow roses, and each evening on his return from a day's hunting they would lighten his sorrow with hugs and kisses.

After a year and a day of deep mourning for his beloved Eve, Lir took the children to see their grandfather, Bov the Red. The gay, cheerful atmosphere of Bov's palace warmed Lir's heart and soon he forgot his terrible loneliness.

Bov was delighted to see the children happy once more, and he suggested that Lir might marry his second daughter, Aoife, who would take the place of the children's mother. Aoife, who was kind and beautiful, agreed, and after the wedding she returned with Lir to Shee Finnaha to take care of the household and the children.

For a time Aoife looked after the children with a mother's love, and they, in turn, cared for their stepmother. But evil touched the heart of Aoife. She became insanely jealous of Lir's love for his children, especially his overwhelming love for the fair-haired Fionnuala, whom he called his 'queen'.

Soon this jealousy turned to hatred. 'Lir loves his children more than he loves me,' Aoife complained, and from that day forth she plotted and schemed to be rid of them.

Early one summer's morning, when Lir was away hunting wild boar, Aoife ordered the horses to be yoked to her chariot

and, with the four children, set out for the palace of Bov the Red. Fionnuala at first begged her brothers not to go. She had sensed Aoife's change of heart and she had dreamed that Aoife was planning to kill them.

But her brothers just laughed at her fears. They longed for the gaiety and noise of Bov's palace. So, very reluctantly, Fionnuala stepped into the chariot. Her fate was sealed.

A white mist was swirling around in a fantastic dance as the horses galloped off. The road wound and curved, and the children were hard set to keep from falling. At each bend in the road Fionnuala looked back as though she knew she would never see her beloved Shee Finnaha again.

The chariot passed through a hamlet, but all the doors were shut and everyone seemed to be in bed. It sped over a bridge and into a little valley.

Suddenly, Aoife stopped the chariot at a small clearing beside Lake Derravaragh.

'Kill the children and you shall be rewarded with silver and gold and wealth untold,' she ordered the charioteer. 'Lir loves his children more than he loves me.'

But the servant drew back in horror, for Lir was a kind and generous master and the children were young and innocent.

'This is a terrible deed you plan, Aoife. Great evil will befall you if you harm Lir's children.'

But Aoife's heart was hardened. If the servant would not do the deed, she would use all her magic powers to rid herself of the children.

She led Fionnuala and her brothers to the shores of Lake Derravaragh and told them to bathe in the water. The morning had turned warm and the boys were glad to frolic in the clear cool waters of the lake, but Fionnuala refused to join them.

'What harm have we done you?' she asked Aoife. 'Lir has enough love in his heart for us all.'

But too late! Already Aoife had lifted her magic wand and had cast a spell on them.

'Out from your home, be swans of Derravaragh's waves.
With clamorous birds begin your life of gloom.
Children shall weep your fate, but none can save,
For I've pronounced the dreadful words of doom.'

Fionnuala gazed at her reflection in the water. Already her neck had grown long. Her golden tresses and her blue gown had turned to feathers. She looked at her brothers. They had changed into snow-white swans. Aoife was still speaking.

'Three hundred years you will spend on Lake Derravaragh, three hundred years on the stormy Sea of Moyle between Ireland and Scotland, and three hundred years on Inis Glora on the wild Atlantic Ocean.

'I will leave you your speech and you will enchant all who hear your sweet, soothing music. The spell will last until you hear the ringing of a Christian bell.'

With that Aoife gave a hollow laugh, swept away in her chariot and left the four swans to their watery fate.

When Aoife arrived at Bov's palace he was disappointed that the children were not with her. Bov was fearful that something terrible had happened to them, and he sent for the charioteer, who told him the story.

Bov was distraught when he heard of Aoife's cruel deed and in black anger he turned his daughter into a hideous demon of the night. With a piercing scream Aoife rose into the air and was never seen again.

The three hundred years the children spent on Lake Derravaragh were strangely happy. Bov the Red built a castle on the shores of the lake and the children were never short of company. Their father, Lir, often came to talk to them. Their fame spread throughout the length and breadth of Ireland and people who were troubled in spirit came to be comforted by their charming music.

But finally the day came when the children had to leave Lake Derravaragh and say goodbye to their family and friends. A hushed silence fell over the lake as Fionnuala spoke for the last time to her beloved father.

'With heavy hearts we must leave the lake we have come to love. We must fly to the Sea of Moyle as our cruel stepmother has decreed. But your love will comfort us during our exile.'

From every corner of the lake huge shoals of trout and pike gathered to say goodbye and overhead great flocks of ducks and geese lined up in formation to fly with the swans as far as the coast.

With a long, lonely cry the swans spread their wings, rose up into the air and flew northwards.

While summer lasted, life was pleasant on the Sea of Moyle. But when winter storms raged and the very waters around them turned to ice, the children suffered greatly. In their worst moments the boys would snuggle close to their sister and she would remind them of happy times at their home at Shee Finnaha before Aoife cast her wicked spell.

When the three hundred years on the Sea of Moyle ended

the Children of Lir took wing and flew south-west to Inis Glora, off the coast of County Mayo. On their journey they flew low over the fort at Shee Finnaha where once they had enjoyed the careless life of happy childhood. But Lir was long since dead and all that remained of their old home was a ruin, all overgrown with weeds and nettles.

Slowly the last three hundred years passed. The waters around Inis Glora were wild and treacherous, but the children were never lonely, for the birds of the air and the creatures of the deep flocked to hear their magical music. The seals did clowning tricks to make the children laugh and the swallows told them strange and wonderful stories of lands across the sea where the sun shone all day and where deserts stretched for thousands of miles.

The seagulls flew inland and brought back news of a holy man called Patrick who had come to Ireland to tell the people about the Christian faith.

Then, one beautiful May morning when the sun was high in the sky, Fionnuala heard the tinkle of a Christian bell.

'It is the bell which will free us,' Fionnuala cried and, with her three brothers, she flew to the shore. There she found Kemoc, one of Patrick's disciples, who listened to their sad story and welcomed them to his chapel. Kemoc told them of Christ and the wonders of heaven. As the holy man prayed with them their white feathers fell away, and instead of four graceful white birds, Kemoc saw before him a very old woman and three withered, feeble old men.

Kemoc baptised them and when they died they were buried in one grave, as Fionnuala had wished — with Conn on her right side, Fiachra at her left and Aodh before her. The holy man knelt to say a last prayer at their grave and as he rose to his feet he saw four beautiful white swans winging their way up into the heavens.

How the Leprechauns Came to Ireland

Leprechauns have been around for thousands of years, but they're not natives of Ireland. Their home is Mag Faithleann, an island off the coast of Ireland, where the wide Atlantic sweeps westwards. They are shoemakers by trade and are said to hide their crocks of gold at the end of the rainbow — or if there are no rainbows around, in some convenient spot. And — if you catch a leprechaun, he *must* tell you where he has hidden his gold!

This is the story of how the first leprechaun came to Ireland and of the bargain that was made with a pair of magic shoes.

Midsummer's Eve was a great festival day in the land of the leprechauns. Iubdan, their King, who used any excuse to celebrate, sent his poet, Eisirt, around his kingdom to invite all and sundry to a party.

Iubdan sat at the top table, with Bebo, his Queen, on his right and Eisirt, his poet, on his left. He was happy. The sun was shining, there was peace and prosperity in the land and the honey drink was the sweetest he had tasted for years.

He clapped his hands for silence and called out, 'Have you ever known a cleverer, a braver or a better king than me?'

With one accord the leprechauns thumped the tables with their fists.

'Never, Never!'

'Have you ever known champions to equal ours in strength and bravery and size?'

'Never, never,' roared the company, the champions shouting louder than the rest.

Glomar, the royal champion, was in his element.

'I am the greatest,' he boasted. 'I can capture a hundred men single-handed with one eye shut and I can hew down a thistle with one stroke of an axe.'

At this Eisirt burst out laughing. 'I never heard such nonsense in all my life,' he cried.

The King was so startled that he almost dropped his goblet of honey wine into the Queen's lap.

'What do you mean?' he thundered, for nobody ever questioned the King.

'I've heard of a place in Ireland, called Emain Macha,' stuttered Eisirt, his confidence fast deserting him, 'where there is a race of giants. Fergus, their King, is the bravest man in the world.'

Some of the leprechauns tittered nervously and at this Iubdan completely lost his temper.

'How dare you speak to your King like that. Guards, to the dungeon with Eisirt.'

Glomar jumped up, but Bebo, the Queen, made him sit down again.

'Be quiet everyone,' she snapped. 'Let the poet explain himself,' for Eisirt was her favourite and she had no wish to cross the little poet. 'Conclude your story,' she said, kindly.

'A ship-wrecked sailor was cast upon the shores of Ireland, Ma'am,' Eisirt continued, 'and barely escaped with his life. He was chased by a fox as big as a house.'

The King smiled sarcastically. 'As you know so much, go to this place called Ireland and bring back proof of your boasting. It will be interesting to hear your story — if you do come back.'

'I shall go to Emain Macha and return within six days,' said Eisirt, 'but when I have brought back the proof you need, then you, King Iubdan, must promise you will make the same journey and taste the king's porridge.' The King agreed. With that, Eisirt stalked out of the palace.

He brushed and cleaned his snow-white horse and rode down to the ocean and out over the waves. In less time than it takes to tell he had reached the shores of Ireland. Dawn was breaking when Eisirt reached Emain Macha, and inside Fergus's fort a new day was stirring.

A great earthen bank surrounded the fort and a guard, wrapped in a rough woollen cloak was asleep beside a wooden gate. Eisirt had never seen such a monstrous creature in his life and it took all his courage to tug at the guard's great cloak.

'I am Chief Poet of the Leprechauns. I command you to take me to King Fergus,' he squealed.

The guard blinked. A little man no bigger than his finger seated on a white horse no bigger than a mouse! He was surely dreaming. Gingerly he picked up the leprechaun and the horse, examined them both from head to toé, then carried them to the King.

King Fergus was sitting at a high table surrounded by his household. Servants were scurrying around with platefuls of delicate food — roast boar, honey cakes, rare wines, rosy apples. Eisirt was scared. He had never, in his wildest dreams, imagined such people. To the tiny leprechaun they looked like giants.

The guard set Eisirt down on the table before the King.

'Here's a visitor from foreign parts, Sire. He says he is a poet. Now tell the company your story, little man.'

'I come from the land of leprechauns,' Eisirt said breathlessly. 'I boasted of how brave and strong the Irish were and our King, Iubdan, ordered me to go to Ireland and bring back proof of my words.'

'Well said,' boomed Fergus. 'Ulster is the strong arm of Ireland. You're a brave wee fellow and deserve our best. Aed, fill our visitor a thimble of mead. We'll drink his health.'

Aed was the King's poet, and although he was the smallest man in Ireland, compared to Eisirt he was a giant.

Aed and Eisirt became firm friends. They swopped poems and stories and when after three days the leprechaun set out on his homeward journey, Aed went with him.

When they reached the west coast of Ireland, Eisirt untied

his little red shoe and threw it into the sea. As soon as the shoe touched the water a white mist rose up from the waves. Then it disappeared and there, rocking on the waves, was a red boat in the shape of a shoe, big enough to hold Aed, Eisirt and the white horse.

The three friends stepped into the boat and in the twinkling

of an eye they had landed at Mag Faithleann. The leprechauns, who had gathered at the water's edge to welcome Eisirt home, scattered in all directions when Aed stood up. But when they saw that Eisirt and the horse were not afraid they crept silently back.

Queen Bebo was sulky. Ever since Eisirt had left she had scolded her husband. Now King Iubdan was so delighted to see the leprechaun and his friend arrive back safely that he declared a national holiday and invited everybody to a banquet.

It was the grandest feast ever held in Mag Faithleann and by the end of the day Eisirt was beginning to feel sorry that he had made his King promise to go to Ireland. But that promise could not be broken, so early next morning, Iubdan set out, accompanied by Bebo, who liked to travel and see the world.

It was very late when they reached Emain Macha and inside the fort all were sleeping. Iubdan and Bebo climbed through a hole in the wall and, following the directions Aed had given them, made their way to the huge kitchens. On the floor was a mighty bronze cauldron. Iubdan stood on a three-legged stool and pulled himself up the side of the pot. He teetered on the edge, overbalanced and found himself waist-high in cold porridge! When Fergus's scullions got up the next morning they discovered Bebo fast asleep beside the cauldron and Iubdan stuck in the thick, lumpy mess.

They brought the pair to Fergus, who ordered the servants to prepare baths for his visitors. That night he gave a banquet in their honour. The feast lasted a year and a day, by which time Iubdan and Bebo had a great wish to return home. But Fergus would not hear of their going. The King and Queen of the leprechauns were his prized possessions and he had no intention of parting with them.

Word reached Mag Faithleann that Iubdan and Bebo were